A PONY AT MOOR END

Wendy Douthwaite

illustrated by
Gavin Rowe

BLACKIE

British Library Cataloguing in Publication Data
Douthwaite, Wendy
A pony at Moor End
I. Title
823'.914[J]   PZ7

ISBN 0-216-91504-X

Blackie and Son Limited
A Member of the Blackie Group
Furnival House, 14/18 High Holborn
London WC1V 6BX

Printed in Great Britain by
McCorquodale (Scotland) Ltd.

Contents

1

Franny Must Go

Sarah woke with a start to find two yellow eyes staring into hers.

"Hallo, Smokey," she mumbled, sleepily. The cat's eyes narrowed to two contented slits and his body reverberated with a deep, continuous purr. Easing herself to a sitting position, being careful not to disturb the sleepy cat, Sarah studied her small bedroom.

It only had a bed and a tall chest of drawers. But, to Sarah it was perfect, with its tiny, cottagey window overlooking the garden. Beyond, stretched field after field, with a backcloth of the Mendip hills behind, purple and misty in the early morning light.

"I *love* it here," Sarah said out loud, partly to herself and partly to Smokey, who kneaded his paws gently at the sound of her voice. "I think it's all so much nicer than Radford House and Clinton," she continued, although by now Smokey was asleep. "I could almost feel *glad* that Dad was made redundant except . . ." Her voice stopped as she glanced at a framed photograph on the chest of drawers. The light strawberry roan pony in the photograph stood with its beautiful, small head held high and its pale mane and tail blowing slightly in the breeze.

Sarah bit her lip and turned her gaze away. No good thinking about Franny now. All *that* had come to an end when Dad had been made redundant over two months ago.

Sarah comforted herself with the thought that she had never quite believed her good fortune at owning her own pony. When Dad had landed a really well-paid executive job and told her that she could have the pony that she had always wanted, for her 10th birthday, she had been almost speechless.

"We'll both ride her," she promised Min, her pony-loving friend from Clinton Primary School, and she kept her promise.

Dad bought a new and larger house with a stable, and Franny was purchased.

"You might as well have a *good* pony while you're about it," Dad had said, as Sarah gazed in awe at the beautiful Franchesca of Ferndene. It wasn't just that Franny had a good pedigree and was a show pony. She also had a beautiful, kind temperament, and Sarah soon loved her more than anything else in the world.

Sarah remembered the day so well, when Dad had told them. It was a Monday in early October. For some reason, school had been closed for the day, so Sarah had gone for a long ride on Franny. Min had gone too, mounted on her old bike. It was a rattly thing, handed down by her three older brothers. By the time it had reached Min, it was bent and battered and held together with cord.

"I suppose it's better than nothing," Min said,

cheerfully, pedalling along beside Franny, imagining herself mounted on a fiery chestnut pony.

Min had left them at the corner of her road, waving goodbye, as her steed wobbled dangerously.

"Woah, Firefly," Min commanded, straightening the handlebars.

Sarah had laughed at her friend's antics as she made her way home to Radford House. It was only three o'clock, but already an evening mist was hanging low over the town. Sarah and Franny turned up to the Avenue, and then down the gravelled drive of Sarah's home.

Sarah put Franny into the stable, offering her a drink of water before going to the garden shed to make up a feed. When Franny heard Sarah coming back with the filled bucket, she whickered softly.

"I know it's really the food you want," Sarah laughed, looking lovingly into Franny's large brown eyes. Franny snorted, eyeing the bucket hopefully and pawing the stable floor impatiently.

Sarah opened the stable door, pushing Franny's enquiring nose away until she was able to put the bucket down in one corner. She stood for a few moments, listening to Franny's contented munching, and breathing in the warm, comfortable smell of the stable.

"See you later, Fran," she had said, at last, letting herself out and bolting the stable door behind her.

As she opened the back door of the house, Sarah was attacked by a bundle of excitement. It was Podge.

"Hey, stop it!" Sarah laughed, fending off Podge's

affectionate licks. He stood, grinning at her, his tail waving and taking most of his body with each wag. Sarah looked at him and grinned back. His name, given to him as a roly-poly puppy, was so unsuitable for such a thin, wiry little dog.

"Is that you, Sarah?" a voice called.

"Yes, Mum. I'm home."

"Cup of tea, dear. We're in the kitchen."

As soon as Sarah opened the kitchen door, she knew that something was wrong. Dad turned a pale and drawn face towards her and Mum's smile was tired and joyless.

"Dad! What are you doing home so early?" Sarah asked.

"Dad's had some bad news," Mum explained. "You're the first one home, so you'll be the first to know."

"I've been made redundant," Dad explained. His voice was flat.

"But . . . what does that *mean?*"

Dad's eyes were dark with misery. "It means," he replied, slowly, "that I'm not needed at work any more. It means that Carson & Co. are having a very bad time at the moment and being the last of the management team to come into the firm, I must be the first to go."

Sarah rushed across and put her arms round her father's neck. "Oh, *poor* Dad," she cried. "How *could* they?"

"They don't have much choice, love," her father replied. "I'm not the only one in the firm to go – there'll be quite a few unhappy homes tonight."

"But – what will it mean for us, Dad. Won't you get another job?"

"It's not quite as easy as that," Mr Hinton explained. "At my age, it's difficult to find work – I was very lucky to get the job in the first place. We'll have to sell up here – a lot of things will have to go." He looked across at Sarah, anxiously, as he said this. "We'll move somewhere much cheaper and live off the redundancy money while I try to find work." He turned towards his wife. "It's very low – the redundancy money – because I've only been with the firm for a year."

Mrs Hinton straightened up. "Look, dear, stop worrying yourself so much. We'll manage somehow, I know we will. I can work, too, you know."

"But will you find work?"

"Of course I will. There's always secretarial work about." She put an arm around Sarah's shoulders. "We'll manage," she repeated, firmly.

Just then, the door burst open and Benny, Sarah's young brother, came tumbling in, eager to tell them all about his day at his friend's house, next door. Next, Peter, the eldest of the three Hinton children arrived home, and soon the whole family knew about Dad's redundancy.

Later on that evening, Sarah slipped away to Franny's stable, where she remained until bedtime. Sarah knew what Dad had meant when he had said "A lot of things must go."

Sitting on her pony's comfortable, warm back, Sarah cried into Franny's mane. She knew only too well that her dear, lovely beautiful Franny must go.

9

2

A New Friend

As Sarah leaned back against her pillow, remembering everything that had happened, it seemed just like a dream.

First, Radford House being put up for sale; then, Dad hearing that his dentist friend, Mr Hughes, was wanting to sell his weekend cottage at Wallington, a village just fifteen miles away.

"It's a bit small – only three bedrooms," Mr Hinton explained, as they all drove out to Wallington to see the cottage.

"We'll manage," Mrs Hinton replied, shouting above the sound of the old car's noisy engine. 'We'll manage' had become her password over the past two weeks. "The boys can share."

"Has it got a field, Dad?" Sarah asked, her mind always on ponies, even though she knew that soon Franny would be gone.

"No, I'm afraid not," Dad answered. "Quite a nice-sized garden, though."

The cottage *was* small, but everyone loved it. Having examined every nook and cranny, Sarah sat on the wide windowsill of the cosy little living room. She opened the window and gazed out across the

fields, marvelling at the quietness, whilst in the background she could hear Benny's feet running excitedly around upstairs.

"Do you like it?" Peter appeared at her shoulder, his grey eyes following her gaze.

"Oh yes," Sarah breathed, "It's lovely. Do you know," she added, wonderingly, "if you sit here and listen, all you can hear is the cows munching the grass in the field across the lane!"

Mr Hughes sold the cottage to Sarah's dad at a bargain price. He had a reason for this. Ever since Debbie, his youngest daughter, who was crazy about ponies, had heard that Franny was to be sold, she had pestered her father.

"So you see, old man," Mr Hughes explained, "If we can include your daughter's pony in the deal, it will make the cottage that much cheaper for you."

On the following weekend, Debbie and her father came to see Franny, and it was arranged that they should take her on a week's approval. Their house, on the other side of Clinton, had stabling and out-houses in the grounds, so there would be no problems in housing a pony.

When the horse-box came, Sarah led Franny carefully up the ramp and into the box. Then, with a last hug, she hurried back down the ramp. Without a word to anyone, Sarah ran indoors and up to her bedroom and there she let the tears come. She had not wanted her father to see her crying, for she knew that selling Franny would help the family situation. They could not possibly afford to keep a pony now, especially one that needed to be stabled.

As expected, Debbie was thrilled with Franny and, before the week's trial had passed, Mr Hughes confirmed that he would be buying the pony.

The move to Dogrose Cottage took Sarah's mind off her loss. For a few days, life was chaotic, with packing cases standing awkwardly in every room. However, life soon settled down. Mum found herself a part-time job at the greengrocers in the village and dad registered at the local Job Centre, studied all the 'Situations Vacant' columns in the newspapers and set to work to dig the garden.

Now, two weeks after the move, Sarah thought of all that had happened and wondered what Christmas, just ten days away, would be like at the cottage. Before she had time to think for very long, the door opened and Benny appeared.

"Can I come in with you?" her tousle-haired brother asked. "Peter says I'm too noisy and he wants to do some Maths." Benny, in his faded blue and white striped pyjamas, smiled at her beguilingly. He shuffled his bare feet on the cold linoleum and shivered exaggeratedly. Sarah grinned and moved over towards the wall. She patted the bed beside her.

"Jump in, you poor, unwanted little creature," she laughed. "Come and keep your toes warm."

Benny climbed in, bringing with him a square, cardboard box.

"Now let's see," said Sarah, "what is it this time – Oh, I remember, beer can rings."

Delightedly, Benny opened the lid of the box and

poured its contents onto the bedspread. Six-year-old Benny was a human magpie. He loved to collect things, and at present his passion was the metal rings from beer and soft drinks cans. Everywhere he went, Benny's eyes searched the ground, the pavements and the hedgerows. Occasionally he pounced delightedly on a new find. A couple of months ago, it had been conkers; rows of conkers had lined all the flat surfaces in Benny's bedroom at Radford House, like a shining army of little, fat brown men.

"Aren't they lovely," said Benny, running his fingers through the metal rings.

"Well, to you, maybe," Sarah replied, doubtfully, wriggling up and out of her bed, "but I must get up. You can stay here if you like and play, but I want to go with Mum when she goes to the shop."

Grabbing her jeans, tee-shirt and sweater from the end of the bed, Sarah made her way down the narrow passage to the bathroom, where she splashed her face with water and pulled on her clothes.

Mum was cooking the breakfast when Sarah arrived in the kitchen.

"Mm they look nice," Sarah said, stealing a slice of frying potato from the pan. "What else is there?"

"Fried eggs," her mother replied. "I bought some from Mrs Potter at the farm." She turned over the potato slices. "You know," she added, "I think we might have a few hens. I don't think they're too expensive to keep."

"Ooh, yes, shall we?" Sarah encouraged, "I'll feed them."

"Well, we'll see what Dad thinks," said Mrs Hinton, spooning out the fried potatoes onto a flat dish. She popped it into the lower oven of the Aga and added some more fat to the frying pan before cracking open the eggs and pouring them into the sizzling fat.

"Shall I call the others?" Sarah asked, "Where's Dad?"

"Yes please," mum replied, "He's in the garden."

"Goodness – already?"

"Mm, I think he enjoys his gardening. We should have our own potatoes next Spring."

"*And* our own eggs," Sarah added. They smiled at each other, conspiratorially, across the kitchen.

The fruit shop was cold and draughty. Sarah explored the dank and smelly depths at the back. Crates of fresh vegetables and fruit, collected earlier that morning from Bristol Fruit Market, were crammed in the back room, waiting to replace the goods in the shop as they were sold.

Sarah tried to help for a while, but the Saturday morning trade was busy. Mrs Hinton and the other assistants worked quickly and efficiently, and Sarah soon found that she was getting in the way instead of helping. She was beginning to wish that she had gone to the library with Peter and Benny, as she settled herself amongst some crates of apples and cauliflowers. She was glad that she had brought some old pony magazines with her, and began to flip through the pages.

After a while, Sarah became aware that she was

being watched. Looking up, she saw a girl of about her own age, peering at her from behind one of the crates.

"Hallo," said the girl. Her brown eyes, beneath an untidy fringe, were friendly. Her long, dark brown hair hung loosely on her shoulders. "My name's Sally," she added.

"There's a huge queue out there," Sally explained, "and I could see your feet sticking out from behind these cases!"

Sarah grinned back at her. "I'm Sarah," she said, "come and join me in my hideout."

Sally squeezed in to sit on the crate beside Sarah, and her eyes fixed delightedly on the magazines.

"Hey! Do you like ponies, too?" she asked.

Sarah nodded.

"Great! I'm crazy about them."

Pulling out a bag from her duffle coat pocket, Sally sealed the friendship with a toffee apiece. She picked up one of the magazines. "Look at that one," she said, pointing to a photograph of a chestnut show pony. "Cassim's that colour, but he's *much* more beautiful." She looked across at Sarah. "He's an Arab," she added proudly.

"Is he yours?" Sarah asked.

"Goodness, no!" Sally laughed. "He's kept at the riding stables where I go to help."

"My pony was part Arab," Sarah said, sadly.

Sally's eyes opened wide. "Did you have your *own* pony?" she asked, incredulously. Sarah nodded. "Phew! You lucky thing. What was it like?"

Sarah described Franny, and told Sally of her

16

dad's redundancy and how they had just come to live in Wallington.

"I haven't seen you at school," Sally said.

"Mum and Dad didn't think it was worth it, just for two weeks," Sarah explained. "We went to our old schools in Clinton for a few days, but then Dad said it was costing too much to travel, and it was almost the end of term anyway."

Changing the subject abruptly, Sally swung round and looked at Sarah. "I'm *so* glad I met you," she said, excitedly. "You can come with me now, on my investigations."

"Investigations?" Sarah echoed, mystified.

"Operation Rescue!" Sally replied, dramatically.

3

Danny

"You can borrow that bike," Sally said, "and I'll use this one." She pulled out two old but serviceable bicycles from the garden shed.

The two girls had explained to their mothers where they were going and had left the fruit shop to go to Sally's house, just round the corner.

"Mum bought the bikes second-hand," Sally explained. "They don't really belong to any of us – we just use them when we want to."

They wheeled the two bikes out of the back yard to a pathway that ran along the back of a row of old-fashioned terraced houses where Sally lived.

"It's not far," Sally explained as they cycled past the sprinkling of small shops and the church which formed the hub of village life at Wallington. They turned down a road just outside the village and pedalled along beside the small river which wound its way quietly across the moors.

"It's funny that I've never seen him before," Sally continued, "but the place is tucked away, down a little lane which doesn't lead anywhere else. I wouldn't have gone last week, only my sister, Julie, has got this paper round after school and I went with her to help her."

Sally stopped and stood with her feet apart, still sitting on the saddle of her bicycle.

"It's down there," she said, pointing down a cinder path, overhung with trees and bushes.

"The path doesn't look as if it's used much," Sarah commented.

"There are only two cottages," Sally explained as they pushed their bikes down the cinder path. "Julie wouldn't wait, so I couldn't investigate." She stopped by a hedge.

"Look! There he is."

Sarah's eyes followed the direction of Sally's pointing finger and she saw a very dejected sight.

The pony's thick brown winter coat could not hide the thinness of his body. He stood by the hedge, close to one of the cottages, his head hanging, miserably.

"Oh, poor little thing," Sarah breathed. "He looks so sad and neglected."

"That's what I thought," Sally said. "I want to have another look at his feet," she added, moving down the hedge towards the gate.

The two girls propped their bikes against the hedge and climbed the gate. They advanced on the little pony, talking to him. He paid little attention to them, just inclining his head very slightly in their direction.

Sally drew in her breath, sharply. "Oh, Sarah, look at them." She pointed to the pony's hooves, cracked and grown long so that they had begun to grow upwards at the front.

"I should think he can hardly walk," Sarah said, her voice filled with concern. "We *must* help him."

"Let's give him the carrots we brought," Sally suggested, "and then we'll try to find out who he belongs to."

The pony took a little more interest when he saw the carrots. He crunched them gratefully and even pushed his velvety black nose into the girls' empty hands when he had finished.

"Poor little pony," Sarah crooned, "we'll bring you some more later."

"Come on," said Sally, tugging at her sleeve. "Let's see if we can find out who owns him."

The pony watched them go, not moving from his position, and then hung his head again, dispiritedly.

A small wooden gate led from the field into the garden of one of the two semi-detached cottages. Sally opened it cautiously. The hinge creaked loudly, and the two girls stopped, guiltily.

"I feel like a burglar," Sarah whispered, as the gate creaked behind them, and they found themselves in a tangle of undergrowth.

"Don't be silly," Sally said, firmly, "we're on an errand of mercy!" Pushing past a clump of dead nettles on the uneven flagged path, she strode purposefully up to the door of the cottage. Lifting the knocker, she banged it loudly. The noise seemed to echo inside the cottage.

"I can't hear anything," said Sally, tilting her head on one side.

"Nor me. Try again."

Sally knocked again. She pushed open the letter

box and peered in.

"It's dark and dingy looking – I can't see much," she reported.

"Shush," Sarah said, "I thought I heard something."

Both girls put their heads close to the letter box and listened. A thin, wavering voice floated out to them. "Come in," it called, "the door's not locked." This was followed by a bout of coughing.

The girls looked at each other.

"Do you think we should?" said Sarah.

"Yes, I think so," Sally replied, after a moment's hesitation, whilst warnings from her mother not to speak to strangers flashed through her mind. "He sounds very old – and not very well." Not waiting to see what Sarah thought, she turned the handle of the door. It squeaked open to reveal the drab hall which Sally had dimly seen through the letter-box. Boldly, Sally stepped inside and peered round the corner, through a doorway on the right.

An old man sat by a coal fire. Round his bent shoulders was draped a bright tartan rug, and another rug covered his knees. He smiled at the two girls as they hesitated in the doorway.

"Come in, do," he said, his old voice cracked and shaky. "Whoever you are. It's good to see someone."

The girls stepped into the room. "We . . . we didn't want to bother you," Sally began, doubtfully.

"My dears, it's good to see someone," the old man repeated, then adding as an afterthought, "but I'm afraid I can't offer you much if you've come carol singing." This set him coughing again, and the girls

22

waited for him to finish.

"Oh no," Sarah insisted, "It's nothing like that – it's the pony in the field next door . . ."

"My little Danny!" The old man's eyes lit up. "He's a nice little fella, aint he? Me and Danny have had some good times together." He paused and stared reflectively into the fire. "We haven't been out in the little cart for a long time, though," he added, sadly. He looked towards the two girls. "Is he all right – my little Danny? Mrs Haines, next door – she looks after him. Makes sure the water trough's got water in it and gives him some peelings and the like." He stared, again, towards the fire. "She's very good to me is Mrs Haines. Does all my shopping, brings me meals. Don't know what I'd do without her . . . Nobody wants an old man nowadays."

The two girls looked at each other. The old man seemed to have forgotten that they were there. Sally stepped forward a pace, into his line of vision.

"He's not really . . . all right," she said, hesitantly.

The old man listened then, as she told him about Danny's split and overgrown hooves and how thin he looked.

"Oh dear, oh dear," he said slowly, when she had finished. "My poor little Danny. What can I do? I can't get out with this wretched bronchitis . . ."

"Shall we look after Danny for you?" Sarah said. The two girls held their breath.

The old man's face brightened considerably. "That would be a load off my mind," he said. He turned and fumbled around on a small table next to his chair. He produced two pound notes and held

23

them out. "Here you are, use this. I've saved it for a present for Mrs Haines, but I reckon my poor little Danny needs it."

Sally hesitated. "Go on, take it," the old man urged. "I can't bear to think of my little Danny like you've told me."

At last, Sally took the two pound notes and pushed them firmly down into the pocket of her jeans. Sarah and Sally looked at each other and grinned, broadly. A pony to look after for Christmas! Both of them were now impatient to leave and begin the care of their new charge.

"Now off you go!" the old man said. "But come back and tell old Bill Codgers how his pony is."

"Can we do anything for you before we go?" Sarah asked. Bill Codgers pulled the tartan rug more tightly around his shoulders and said, "Well, my dears, if you could just put a few more lumps of coal on the fire . . . if I get up to do it myself, it starts off my cough."

This done, the two girls said goodbye, leaving Bill Codgers by his cheerful fire. Closing the front door carefully behind them, they ran down the path to where the little pony still stood. He raised his head hopefully as the girls hurried over.

"We're going to look after you, Danny," Sarah told him, stroking his thickly coated neck.

"And we'll get those feet seen to as soon as we can," Sally promised, rubbing him behind his ears. "We can't stay now," she added to Sarah. "It's nearly 1 o'clock – let's go home now and meet at my house after dinner."

4

Moor End

"The main problem is – we're going to need some money."

Sally was sprawled at one end of her bed, whilst Sarah sat at the other, swinging her legs over the side. Sally's bedroom, shared with her fifteen-year-old sister, Julie, was not large. The room was divided by a double-sided unit of shelves and drawers. Sally's side was dotted with horses in various forms – china, plastic and wood – with a photograph of Cassim in pride of position. On Julie's side, make-up, brushes, combs and a hair-dryer littered the shelves.

"She just sits there all day, combing her hair and sighing," Sally complained, "*and* she's got the window. I have to have my light on all the time. It's awful, having to share."

"She isn't here now," Sarah pointed out.

"Ah, yes," Sally agreed, "but any minute now, she'll unwind herself from the settee, where she's draped, watching the telly, and then she'll be up, combing and glaring at herself and pulling faces in the mirror!"

Sarah laughed at her new friend's exaggerated

talk. "You should try being a girl in the middle of two boys!" she retorted.

"What are they like?"

"Well, they're not too bad, I suppose," Sarah admitted, thinking of her two very different brothers. Six-year-old Benny's high spirits were easy to understand, but Peter . . . Peter was very bright – too bright for his own good, dad said. At times, he was so quiet and withdrawn that the other members of the family found it difficult to communicate with him. At other times, he was full of fun and would tease Sarah and Benny unmercifully.

Sarah sighed. "Funny things – families," she said, simply. "But we still haven't thought about our problem – money!"

"Mmm." Sally frowned. "I just haven't got *any,*" she said, "not to spare, that is. I've still got a pound left, but I haven't bought dad's Christmas present yet."

"I'm the same," Sarah admitted, "Still, we *have* got the £2 from Mr Codgers – what shall we spend that on?"

Sally frowned again. "I'm *sure* it will cost more than that to have Danny's hooves cut back," she said. She sat up, suddenly. "I know," she said, "let's go to Moor End." Sarah looked at her, questioningly. "The riding stables," Sally explained. "I can show you Cassim, and we can ask Mandy for the blacksmith's telephone number."

The yard at Moor End Riding Stables seemed to be full of ponies and people as Sarah and Sally cycled over the small stone bridge and past a white-washed cottage, the lawn of which ended at the riverside.

"That's where Mandy lives," Sally said, glancing towards the cottage. "That's Mandy, there," she added, pointing to a young woman dressed in jodhpurs and a yellow polo-necked sweater.

"She looks very young."

Sally laughed. "She just *looks* younger than she is," she said. "That's Rob over there – her husband." A young man with curly brown hair was giving a plump little girl a leg up into the saddle.

Propping their bikes against the side wall of the cottage, Sally and Sarah hurried over to Mandy. She was leading a beautiful chestnut pony from one of the stables. Sarah recognised Cassim from the photograph in Sally's bedroom, and her heart turned over when she looked at the beautiful Arab head, so like Franny's except for the colour.

"Hallo, Sally," Mandy said, smiling. "Have you come to help?"

"Well, not exactly," Sally replied. "We wondered – Oh, this is my friend, Sarah. She's come to live at Dogrose Cottage."

Mandy turned from tightening the girth. She smiled at Sarah.

"You're *living* there, are you?" she asked. Sarah nodded. "Oh, that's good," Mandy Walters continued. "I always think it's such a shame when cottages stand empty for most of the year. It doesn't help village life."

Sarah smiled back into Mandy's cheerful face. "I *love* it there," she said.

27

"Good. Then let's hope you'll be staying. What can I do for you two, then? We'll be off on the three o'clock ride soon."

Sally explained the reason for their visit. Mandy looked concerned when she heard about Danny's feet. "I had no idea," she said, as she leapt lightly into the saddle. Moving her knee forward, she lifted the saddle flap and again tightened the girth strap. The chestnut shook his head and snorted loudly.

"He blows out, the naughty thing," Mandy laughed, patting Cassim's neck, affectionately. "Now I come to think of it," she continued, "I haven't seen old Bill Codgers for ages." She looked down, thoughtfully. "I tell you what, Sally," she said. "I should think that pony of his needs some proper food and some hay. There can't be much grass in that little field of his, now. You say Mr Codgers gave you £2?" Sally nodded. "Well, you can buy a bale of hay from me, if you like, for £1 – that's what I paid for it. Take a bale with you, and take him a feed from the feed room, just to start him off. Then you can buy some pony nuts with your other pound." She frowned. "I'm afraid old Bill Codgers shouldn't really be keeping a pony now. He's only got his old age pension, and besides, he isn't well enough to look after it properly."

"Well, we're going to help him now, as much as we can, said Sally."

Mandy smiled again. "Good luck," she said. "Oh – I nearly forgot. When I come back, I'll telephone Tom Brigsley, the blacksmith, and ask him if he can fit Danny in on Thursday. He's coming over here to

shoe three of mine, and I expect he'll be able to cut Danny's feet back then."

"But what will he charge?" Sally asked, looking worried.

The ponies were all ready to go. Mandy began to move off, Cassim stepping lightly across the yard.

"I would have thought no more than £5," Mandy called. "Will that be all right? I'll pay Tom for all of them together, if you like, and you can pay me back."

Waving, Mandy led the ride out of the yard and across the bridge, turning right on to the lane which led across the moors. Cassim, leading the ride, seemed to float down the lane, prancing slightly, his long, straggly Arab tail held high.

Sarah and Sally looked at each other and grinned.

"All we have to do now," Sally said, "is find some money!"

"It's not as easy as it sounds – having a pony to look after," said Sarah.

"It's lovely to think of him there, though, isn't it – almost as if he belongs to us!"

Sally led the way to the feed room. "We'll have to see if Mr Codgers has a bucket, but we'll borrow one for now," she said. "Mandy won't mind."

"She's nice, isn't she?" Sarah said. "And Cassim is gorgeous, isn't he?"

Sally paused, one hand holding the bucket and the other about to plunge into the bin of crushed oats. "He *is*," she said, dreamily. "He's the most beautiful pony I've ever seen." Sally turned towards her friend, her eyes shining. "One day, I'm going to have stables, like Mandy's, and by that time perhaps Mandy won't need Cassim any more, and then I'll be able to buy him. He's a stallion, you know," she added, importantly. "And Mandy wants to breed Arabs. She's got to run the riding stables to make money so that she can buy some really good mares." Sally continued to put handfuls of food into the bucket, mixing oats, bran, flaked maize and pony nuts together. "There, I think that's plenty. We can mix it with water at the field. Now we'll go and fetch the hay."

Sarah rested a bale of hay on the handlebars of her bike. Sally hung the bucket over hers, and they wheeled their two bikes across the bridge and back along Moor Lane towards the village. The cinder path leading to Bill Codgers' cottage was not far down the lane from the riding stables, and soon they saw Danny, standing next to the hedge, his head hanging, dejectedly.

This time, he lifted his head and watched intently as they approached.

"He knows us already," Sarah said, delightedly.

Leaving the bucket of food in the old shed next to the cottage, the two girls lifted the bale of hay onto the floor and pulled off the twine that tied it.

"If we eke it out, it should last for ages," Sally said, pulling a section away.

"That doesn't look very much," Sarah said, doubtfully, remembering the armfuls of hay that she had stuffed into Franny's hay-net.

"Mm, I know, but it'll look much more when we shake it out," Sally pointed out, "and he's not *work-*

ing, remember – just standing in his field all day." She picked up the hay in her arms. "And he's going to have his feed, too," she said. "Have you got the brushes?" she added.

Sarah dived for her saddle bag and brought out Franny's grooming tools. When Franny had been sold, Sarah had kept most of her horsey equipment. Many of the things had been presents last Christmas and, anyway, she liked having them. Somehow, just *seeing* the dandy brush and tail comb helped to ease the ache when she thought of Franny.

The two girls spent a contented hour brushing the mud from Danny's dense brown coat, and combing his long-neglected mane and tail, which were tangled and full of burrs. Meanwhile, Danny munched happily at the hay.

Sarah brushed Danny's withers, thoughtfully. "I wonder if we could ride him?" she said.

Sally straightened up. "I've been wondering that, too," she admitted. "But we haven't got a saddle or bridle."

"No . . o," Sarah admitted, "but I've got Franny's headcollar and leading rope at home."

They looked at each other across Danny's back.

"Perhaps when his feet are better and he's not so thin, we could ask Mr Codgers," Sally suggested. "How high do you think Danny is?"

"About 12.2, I should think."

"That's what I thought."

Danny snorted contentedly into his hay as the two friends bent their heads again to their work, each planning expeditions with their new charge.

5

Making Money

"If you're going to stay there all day, you might as well help me!" Mrs Hinton looked across the kitchen at her daughter with amusement in her eyes. "You've been sitting there, frowning and sighing for the last quarter of an hour," she laughed. "What's the matter?"

Sarah looked up. "I just wish I could think of how to get some money!" she sighed.

With floury hands, Sarah's mum pushed over two baking tins. "Just grease these two, will you, love? Then you can cut out some pastry rounds with the cutters, and put them in the tins, while I roll out some more pastry. I'm making mince pies." She began to wield the rolling pin again. "Now, what do you need money for – as if I didn't know!"

Sarah frowned. "Well, it's just that Danny needs feeding up for a while – he's so thin. And then, we've got to pay for his feet, and he'll need hay until about April. I don't know how Sally and I can manage. We *want* to look after him for Mr Codgers, but . . ." Her voice trailed away, miserably.

"Mm. A bit of a problem," Mrs Hinton agreed. "Really, it sounds as though the old man should sell his pony if he can't afford to keep it properly."

"But, you see, Mum," Sarah broke in, "if only Sally and I can look after him this winter, he won't need feeding in the summer, and perhaps we can ride him."

"But he hasn't a saddle or bridle, has he?" said Mrs Hinton.

"Well, I don't *think* so," replied Sarah, "but he must have some kind of bridle – Mr Codgers used to put him in a trap."

Mrs Hinton continued to roll the rolling pin back and forth, thoughtfully.

"Well," she said, slowly, "this Mandy you told me about – maybe she might borrow Danny in exchange for some food for him. You said that she has more children wanting to ride at weekends and doesn't have many ponies."

Sarah's face brightened. "That's a good idea, Mum – we could ask Mandy. The trouble is," she added, doubtfully, "we don't even know what Danny's like to ride, and he needs a while to get his strength back, and we need money to feed him *now*, and for his feet." She paused for breath and looked at her mother hopefully.

"Let's think again, then," said Mrs Hinton. "Perhaps there's something you can do . . . something to do with Christmas.

"What sort of thing?"

"I'm just thinking . . ." mum replied.

There was a silence for a while in the warm little kitchen. Sarah fitted the rings of pastry into the baking tins whilst her mother paused to concentrate.

"I'm sure somebody . . ." she said slowly. "I know!" she cried, triumphantly.

Sarah looked expectant, as her mother continued. "Mrs Crudge at the fruit shop was complaining yesterday that people were asking her if she had any holly, and she said there wasn't any at the market and she didn't know where to get any."

A mischievous smile spread over Mrs Hinton's face. "But *I* know where to get some," she said, smugly.

"Mum!" Sarah's eyes were shining. "You're full of marvellous ideas! Where is it?"

".Just up in the woods behind the farm. I saw it last Sunday when I took Podge for a walk – there's plenty of it!"

"But would it be all right just to take it?" Sarah questioned.

"You'll have to ask Mr Potter. Those woods are part of his farm land, but I don't think he bothers with them. I'm sure he wouldn't mind – go and ask him."

"Mum, you *are* clever." Sarah fitted the last pastry round into its place in the tin. "How much do you think Mrs Crudge will pay for the holly, if Mr Potter lets us pick it?"

"She said that shops in Bristol were charging 40p a bunch, but that she would charge 30p – I expect she would pay you about 15p a bunch.

Sarah counted quickly on her fingers. "That would be nearly a pound for six bunches. Gosh! That would be great."

"Now, steady," Mrs Hinton laughed. "Don't strip

35

the woods completely, will you. And don't count your chickens before they're hatched – you might be disappointed if it doesn't all work out."

Sarah's mind was distracted for a moment by her mother's words. "What about the hens, Mum – what did Dad think?"

Mrs Hinton began spooning mincemeat into the pastry cases, "He thought it was a good idea, but he didn't think we could afford them just now – the house and pen will cost quite a lot, even second-hand." She opened another pot. "All the big bills come in straight after Christmas, you know – rates, electricity and suchlike."

A sudden feeling of guilt spread over Sarah. She was busy worrying about money to feed someone else's pony, whilst Mum was worrying about money to pay the bills.

"Oh dear," she said, slowly, "perhaps I could sell the holly to help with the bills." She faltered, thinking of Danny's thin flanks.

Mrs Hinton put an arm around her daughter's shoulders. "Now look, love, we'll pay the bills – don't you worry. You and Sally are helping an old man." She smiled. "I know it's no hardship to you, looking after a pony, but you're helping someone *and* a neglected pony as well. Old Mr Codgers sounds as though he is very fond of his pony. I think it's nice that you two are going to look after Danny whilst he's ill."

The door-bell rang and Sally arrived in the kitchen. Sarah told her of mum's idea.

"Let's go and see Mr Potter now," she said,

"then, if he says yes, we can go hollying this afternoon!"

"My hands hurt," Benny wailed. His eyes were brimming with tears.

"Poor little Ben," Sarah said, soothingly, examining his holly-pricked hands. "You've been lots of help, you really have," she added encouragingly. "Now look," she said, pulling her little brother over towards a fallen log and pushing him down to a sitting position. "You just sit here and guard the sledge, while we pick a bit more holly." She rummaged around in her pocket. "Here you are," she said, bringing out a somewhat delapidated-looking sweet. "I *thought* I had one of Sally's toffees in there, somewhere."

Placated temporarily by the toffee, Benny waited on the log, while Sarah returned to the holly bush, where Sally and Peter were busy. Peter clipped the stems and handed the prickly branches carefully down to Sally, who put them gingerly on top of the pile, already picked. She stopped to suck her stinging fingers as Sarah approached.

"I don't blame Benny," she said, ruefully, "I never realised quite how prickly holly was."

Sarah picked up the string and scissors and resumed her job of tying the branches together into bunches. "Just think of all those pony nuts," she said, cheerfully, "and Danny's feet when they're cut back".

"I'm trying to – ouch!"

"Maybe we've got enough for now," Sarah

suggested, "I've tied up twenty nine bunches, so far."

Peter paused and peered at them through the holly bush. "That's £4.35," he said.

"Shall we stop, then?" Sally asked, hopefully. "There's quite a lot here that you haven't bunched yet."

"And I'm hungry," Peter pointed out from the bush.

"Come on then, you faint-hearted lot!" Sarah laughed. "Help me with this bunching and then we can go home for tea."

Podge appeared from hunting in the undergrowth, and then Benny arrived, trailing the sledge. "It's all creepy and spooky," he complained, "and I'm hungry."

"I don't know why we brought you," Peter grumbled, impatiently, and Benny began to cry.

"Oh, Pete, don't be so mean. It *is* a bit dark and creepy in these woods," said Sarah.

"Sorry I spoke," Peter snapped.

"Oh dear," Sally looked from one to the other. "*Please* don't quarrel. I think we're all a bit tired and hungry." She shivered. "It's cold now, too, isn't it?"

"Perhaps it's going to snow," Peter suggested, brightening up.

Cheered a little by this thought, the four tired holly-pickers decided to forego the rest of the bunching and to pile the spare holly onto the sledge and tie it down with the string.

"How are we going to manage all those?" Sally asked, pointing towards Sarah's pile of neatly-bunched holly.

"We can carry some," said Peter, "and . . ." He thought for a moment. "We can tie the others to our belts. Come on – let's do Sally first!"

"I feel ridiculous!" Sally said, when the others had finished tying the holly bunches round her waist. "Like a walking holly bush!"

"I haven't got a belt!" wailed Benny.

"It's all right, Benny," Sarah said, hastily. "We can tie them to your little straps at the side – see?" She fixed two bunches before Benny had time to argue. Sarah and Peter tied bunches of holly to each other, and they all gathered the rest in their hands.

"Who's going to pull the sledge?" Sally asked.

"I will," Peter volunteered, manoeuvring the sledge rope in amongst the holly in his right hand.

They set off, out of the wood and across the field in a straggling line, with Benny and Podge trailing at the back.

Sally giggled. "If we meet anyone on their way home from their Sunday afternoon walk," she said, "they'll think they're seeing things. We must look like a walking wood!"

6

The Sale

The next morning, Sarah and her mother walked to the fruit shop, carrying twelve bunches of holly.

"Better not take too many," Mrs Hinton said.

Much to Sarah's relief, Mrs Crudge at the shop seemed delighted and paid Sarah £1.80. "Judging from the enquiries I've had," she told Sarah, "I should be able to take some more from you soon."

Sarah could hardly wait for the afternoon, when Sally had arranged to call in on her way home.

"I wish school would hurry up and finish," Sally complained, resting her satchel on the kitchen floor. "How did you get on with the holly?"

Sarah produced the £1.80 and told her what Mrs Crudge had said. "I bunched up the rest of the holly," she said, "and we've still got 25 bunches."

"Marvellous," Sally said, warmly. "We can buy some pony food now."

Sarah looked up at the kitchen clock. "Have we got time to go this evening, do you think?" she said. "We haven't given Danny his hay yet."

"We – ll," Sally replied, doubtfully, "I don't know about you, but I don't think Mum would let me cycle back from Nelfield in the dark, and the light's fading already."

"We could go by bus," Sarah suggested.

"Mm. But that would cost us 50p each – nearly half our money."

Mrs Hinton joined in at this stage. "I tell you what, girls. Let's be very extravagant and take the car, just for once. There are one or two things that I need for the church sale on Wednesday, and I can't buy them in Wallington. We'll call by at your house, Sally, and tell your mother where you are. Then we can pop in on the way to give Danny his hay."

At the pet shop in Nelfield, huge bins of various types of corn and pet foods lined the walls at the back of the shop. The girls bought 7lb bags of pony nuts, flaked maize, oats and bran, which cost all of the £1.80, plus the pound from Bill Codgers.

"That's all our money gone, now," Sarah said. "Let's hope Mrs Crudge wants some more holly."

"I've been thinking about nothing else but earning money today," Sally told her, as they wandered around the shop, peering in at the guinea pigs and rabbits. "Mrs Pilkington kept telling me off for day-dreaming!"

"We'll just have to keep on thinking," said Sarah.

"At least we've got some pony food now," Sally pointed out. "And if we sell all the holly, maybe we'll have enough for Danny's feet."

Sarah stopped suddenly. "Mistletoe!" she shrieked excitedly.

The rabbits stopped chewing to stare at her with round eyes, and an old woman buying canary seed jumped, nearly dropping her change.

"Good Morning!" squawked a Mina bird from his cage, in response, and Sally began to giggle.

"Don't you *see*," Sarah said, impatiently, lowering her voice, "we can sell that, too. I've just remembered. I'm sure I saw some in the orchard when we went to ask Mr Potter about picking the holly."

"Mr Potter might say no this time," Sally reminded her.

"Well, we can always ask – look, there's mum. We'd better go."

As the two girls made for the door, carrying their parcels, the Mina bird peered down at them with beady eyes and shrieked, "Good morning! Good morning!" Sally was overcome by a fit of giggles, and they both arrived outside the shop in the cold December air, weak at the knees with laughing.

Although it was the largest room in the house, the living room at Dogrose Cottage was small. Still, Sarah thought from her favourite position, curled up on the plump cushions in the window-seat, that only made it all the more cosy; especially when the fire was lit and the logs which dad had sawn crackled and sparked cheerily in the grate. This evening, Sally was with her in the window-seat. Mrs Hinton had called in at Sally's house on the way home, and arranged that she could stay for the evening.

"We'll walk home with her at 9 o'clock," Mrs Hinton had promised Sally's mother.

After town life, with its street lamps and neat, tree-lined roads, the newly-countryfied Hinton family enjoyed walking through the lanes at night.

Somehow, the country stars seemed to shine and shimmer more brightly and the country air was sharper and cleaner.

Mrs Hinton was sewing, whilst Dad was reading the evening paper. Benny busily lined up his rings on the hearthrug, where Podge lay, lost in his paw-twitching dog dreams. Peter was sprawled on the settee, reading.

Sarah looked out at the blue-black sky with its twinkling stars. She liked this time between afternoon and evening, when there was still a slight after-glow where the sun had set two hours earlier. She thought of Danny, munching his hay in his field down on the moors.

"What shall we give Danny for Christmas?" she asked Sally, breaking the silence.

Sally looked startled. "I – hadn't really thought," she admitted, "I can't afford anything, really."

"We could make a carrot Christmas pudding," Sarah suggested.

Sally giggled. "With a piece of holly on top," she chuckled.

Sarah turned to give her a withering look, but then she, too, began to laugh. "I wonder how Mrs Crudge got on with our holly," she said, when they had calmed down.

"Don't forget to ask about the mistletoe tomorrow – I can help you pick it after school, if Mr Potter agrees," Sally reminded her.

"Mm. OK."

Sally drew her knees up under her chin. "Just think," she said happily, "only two more days at school, and then two weeks of freedom."

"And then I'll be coming to school, too."

"Great!"

Sarah looked down at Benny on the hearthrug. "You must have *hundreds* of those things," she said to him, looking at the rings. "How many are there in your box?"

Benny looked back, cheekily. "Shan't tell you!" he retorted.

"All right then, we'll guess," Sally returned.

"Three hundred and twenty," Sarah suggested.

Benny rolled about on the hearthrug with delight. "No!" he chuckled. This was a good game.

This time Sally tried. "Five hundred and two," she said.

Benny shrieked with laughter, shaking his head vigorously.

"We could go on like this for ever," Sarah sighed.

Mum looked up from her sewing. "I think I've had another idea for your money-making project," she said.

Sally and Sarah listened, hopefully.

"You could persuade Benny to lend you his precious rings," she began, looking down with a smile at her small son, "put them in a jar – one of those old sweet jars I've got would do – and have a 'Guess the number of rings' competition. All you'll need is a prize for the winner – and you can hold the competition at the Church Sale on Wednesday," Mum finished triumphantly.

Sarah and Sally looked at each other, delightedly. Things were looking up!

"I had a letter from Min, today!" Sarah shouted, as she and Sally sped down the hill on their bikes, towards the moors. Sally had finished school early, and it was still daylight.

"Who?" Sally called.

"My friend from Clinton!"

They slowed a little as they reached the flatter road which led to the heart of the village. They turned left into Moor Lane and the pace slowed as they pedalled along beside the knarled spiky-headed Willows, which leaned at crazy angles over the little river.

"I told you about Min," Sarah continued, "Well, she's coming over after Christmas, and mum said she can stay for the night."

They stopped at the beginning of the cinder path and pushed the bikes over the pot-holed path. Sarah pulled out a letter from the pocket of her jeans.

"She says," Sarah said, reading from the letter, "Debbie has been hunting on Franny, and Franny is looking very fit . . ." Sarah stuffed the letter back into her pocket and kicked at a stone, moodily.

Sally looked at her, sympathetically. "It must be awful, knowing that someone else owns Franny now," she said.

"I just mustn't think about it," Sarah sighed, partly to herself.

A whicker from the field turned Sarah's attention from thoughts of Franny, and she hurried to help Sally with the mixing of Danny's feed.

Leaning an arm on Danny's withers while he munched the contents of his bucket, Sally said,

"We'll go and see Mandy, shall we, after we've been to see Mr Codgers, and find out what time the blacksmith is coming on Thursday."

"You'll be on holiday then, won't you?" Sarah said, and Sally nodded. "Perhaps we could try riding Danny," She looked at the pony's inviting back. "I haven't ridden for *ages*," she added, wistfully.

"There's certainly plenty to do in the country," Sarah informed Smokey, who had followed her upstairs and was busy finding himself a comfortable place on her bed. Finally, satisfied, he curled himself up into a tight ball, wrapping the tip of his tail neatly over his grey nose. "It's all right for you," Sarah grumbled, zipping up her skirt, "you've only got one set of clothes — mum can't make *you* change!"

It was Wednesday, the day of the Church Sale. The Sale was a family affair and so it was held in the evening. Mrs Hinton had insisted that Sarah should change from her muddy, Danny-smelling jeans into a skirt, clean sweater and long socks.

Mum's voice floated up the stairs, "Come on, everyone, we don't want to be late!"

The Hintons made their way down the moonlit lane to the village, calling in at Sally's house, where Sally and her family joined them. Light spilled out of the Church Hall, the doors of which were open wide for the evening. The Sale was to be a big social occasion in the village.

Sally's mother had asked permission from the vicar for the two girls to run their competition from the soft toy stall, which she and Mrs Hinton were

46

running. The sweet jar, filled with Benny's rings, was placed in a prominent position, together with the notice which Sarah had written, 'Guess the number of rings and win a prize – 5p per go.' Sarah waited, hopefully, with paper and pen, while Sally wandered about the room looking for suitable customers. She returned almost immediately with a tall, middle-aged man, who peered down at Sarah, shortsightedly. This was Mr Peterson, the vicar.

"Well now, 5p a go," said the vicar. "That's very reasonable. I'll start you off with two goes." He thought for a moment, studying the jar. "Let's say six hundred and eighty-five and . . . seven hundred and nine." When Sarah had written down his name and guesses and taken his 10p, Mr Peterson said, "I hear that you are helping to look after Mr Codgers' pony. How is the old man?"

"He hasn't much money," Sally began, "and he's ill."

"And he seems very lonely," Sarah added.

Mr Peterson nodded in the slow, deliberate way of vicars. "Well," he said, beginning to move off, "we must do something about that."

The competition went well, giving the two girls little time to see the rest of the Sale.

"Just as well, really," Sally remarked, "I haven't any spare money, anyway."

Later on, Mandy came to try her luck and they told her what the competition was in aid of. "You *are* doing well," she said, warmly, when she heard of their progress so far. "Don't forget tomorrow," she added, "twelve o'clock."

7

A Pony to Ride

"There we are, then," said the blacksmith, straightening up and giving Danny a friendly slap on the quarters. "He should feel more comfortable now."

Danny now stood on neat little hooves, expertly cut back and trimmed. "He's got good hard feet," Tom Brigsley commented. "You might get away without shoes unless you intend to ride a lot. That'll be £3," he added as he packed his tools into the back of his van."

When Tom Brigsley had driven off down the path, Sally and Sarah looked at each other, delightedly.

"We've got £2 left," Sally said.

"And more holly and mistletoe left to sell," Sarah added, happily. "Let's take Danny for a walk – I brought the headcollar."

"We'll go and ask Mr Codgers first, though, shall we?" Sally looked towards the cottage. "I wonder . . ." she mused.

"What?"

"Well, I think we could take Danny round to the side of the cottage and if we opened the curtains, Mr Codgers could look out and see him."

"Oh yes, he'd like that, wouldn't he."

Sarah fetched the headcollar and leadrope from the saddlebag on her bike and fitted it round Danny's head. "It's a bit big," she said, "but it fits."

Leading the little pony carefully through the small gate, they guided him round the overgrown flower beds and stopped by the living room window at the side of the house, where the curtains were drawn to keep in the warmth. Danny, who had not been out of his field for a long time, snorted and shied at every new object he saw.

"He looks a different pony with his head held up like that and his ears pricked," Sally said, patting his neck, fondly. "He's really very pretty, isn't he?"

Sarah, like Sally, felt excited at the prospect of a pony to ride, even just bareback and with a headcollar. "He's gorgeous," she agreed. "I'll go and tell Mr Codgers."

Knocking first, Sarah pushed open the front door of the cottage and called out, "It's only me – Sarah!"

In the warm living room, old Mr Codgers sat by his fire. He was pleased to hear about the blacksmith.

"And you've got my little Danny outside, have you?" he said. "Pull back the curtains then, little Missie," he said, his old voice tinged with excitement. Sarah pulled back the curtains with a flourish, to reveal Danny, who peered in at them, his wayward mane falling untidily about his pricked ears.

There were tears in the old man's eyes as he turned towards Sarah. "I haven't seen my little Danny for months," he told her. "That's a good Christmas present, to see him and to know that you

two girls are looking after him."

"He's looking better already, after the hay and food, and he can walk properly now," Sarah told him. She hesitated. "We wondered . . ."

The old man's eyes were twinkling now. "You wondered if you could ride him," he said, "well, of course you can. He needs something to do. And now I've got something for you." He turned round in his chair and pointed to the old sofa. "I asked Mrs Haines to fetch that out of the scullery for me, as a surprise for you two girls."

On the sofa was a heap of old harness. Sarah could see a headpiece and snaffle bit, and reins which seemed to go on for ever. There were other strange pieces of leather and straps. She fingered it, excitedly; it felt dry and cracked.

"It needs some cleaning," the old man said, "but I think you'll be able to make a bridle from it. You'll find some neatsfoot oil in a tin in the shed. That should make the leather much softer."

"Can we really use it?" Sarah asked, excitedly. "We'll clean it all for you, Mr Codgers."

The old man smiled happily, looking back towards Danny, who was nibbling at some weeds which grew around the window. "It's so good to see my little Danny again," he murmured. The excitement had tired him and his eyes began to close.

"You know, what Mr Codgers needs is another pet – one that he can have indoors with him," Sally remarked.

"Like a dog, or something?"

51

"Mm. But he can't take a dog for walks, can he?"

The two girls were sitting on the kitchen floor of Sally's home. Newspapers were spread over the floor and they were surrounded by pieces of harness.

"I hope we can fit it all together again," Sally said, rubbing neatsfoot oil vigorously into a strap.

"'Course we will!"

"What about a cat?" Sally suggested.

"Ye – es," Sarah agreed, doubtfully, "but they have to be let in and out all the time, and Mr Codgers can't really do that, either."

Sally thought for a while. "What about that Mina Bird in the pet shop?" she suggested.

"They're so expensive, though."

"Well then, a budgie. They don't cost all *that* much and they're good company."

Sarah looked up from the bit which she was cleaning in warm water. "That would be just right," she admitted, "but I don't know why we're talking about it – we can't afford to buy one."

"What a shame," Sally sighed, "a budgie would be lovely company."

The two girls worked in dedicated silence for a while. The dry leather now felt soft and supple. They fitted the pieces of the bridle together again, buckling just one of the two long driving reins to the rings on either side of the snaffle bit.

"There," said Sally triumphantly, "a bridle for Danny!"

"We could go for a quick ride," Sarah pointed out excitedly. "It's only half past two."

"Great idea," Sally agreed.

"Where shall we go?"

"Not too far, I suppose."

Danny, wearing his newly-cleaned bridle, and with Sally astride his bare back, waited eagerly. He was as excited as the two girls.

"I've been thinking," Sally said, slowly. "Perhaps the vicar might help."

"It's all that polishing," Sarah confided to Danny. "It's sent her round the bend. How on earth can the vicar help us to decide where to go?" she questioned.

"No, stupid. I mean about the budgie for Mr Codgers. He did say that he wanted to help him, didn't he? Let's go round and see him – it's not far."

It was Mrs Peterson who opened the door of the old vicarage. "I'm afraid my husband's not in," she told the two girls, when Sally explained the reason for their visit. "But why don't you come in a minute – you can put the pony in one of those sheds."

Sally slid down from Danny's back and led him over to one of the vicarage outhouses. She found an old, empty stable and left Danny there, first taking off his bridle and hanging it on a hook outside. He watched Sally leave, his little brown head only just managing to look out through the upper opening of the stable door.

Mrs Peterson had left the outer front door open, and Sally found Sarah in the huge vicarage kitchen. She was sitting on a stool by the stove, eating a slab of fruit cake.

"Come on, Sally," said Mrs Peterson, offering her the cake tin, "I'm sure you can do with something to

53

eat on a cold day like this. Sarah has been telling me about your idea for old Mr Codgers and I'm going to talk to my husband tonight. It's just what that old man needs, I'm sure. We are going to take him some Christmas foods, using some of the proceeds of the Sale." She looked at them, seriously. "You've got to be careful, though," she added. "Country people are sometimes very proud and they don't like to think they're accepting charity."

Sally devoured the fruitcake. "Do you think the budgie is a good idea?" she asked, between mouthfuls.

"I most certainly do," Mrs Peterson replied. "I was talking to Mrs Haines last night at the Sale – did you do well with your competition, by the way?"

Sarah nodded. "We made nearly £5 profit," she replied, proudly. "We can buy Danny some more hay now, and pony food."

"Oh good." Mrs Peterson went back to her previous topic. "Mrs Haines tells me old Bill Codgers has a son living in Bristol who hardly ever goes to see him – poor old man. Never mind, we'll give him a good Christmas. Will you help us take things round to his home on Christmas Eve?"

"Oh yes," they agreed.

"It'll have to be in the morning," Mrs Peterson mused, "because Jack will be busy later on."

"Sally looked out of the window, where dusk was darkening the sky. "We'd better be going," she said, standing up. "Thanks for the cake, Mrs Peterson."

"Come and see me tomorrow then," said Mrs Peterson, as she let them out. She shivered. "It's getting colder – I think it might snow for Christmas."

8

The Accident

Sarah's Christmas began at 6 o'clock in the morning on Christmas Eve, when Benny appeared in her bedroom, jiggling up and down with excitement.

"It's snowing! It's snowing! Come and look!"

"Go back to bed, Benny – it's not Christmas Day yet," Sarah mumbled from the warm cocoon of her bed.

But Benny was not to be put off so easily, and soon Sarah, too, was standing, shivering, and peering out at the white flakes which cascaded past her window.

Later on that morning, there was the trip to old Bill Codgers' house, with Sally and the Petersons. The two girls had helped Mrs Peterson to choose a cheeky green budgerigar from the pet shop in Nelfield, and the vicar had managed to acquire an old bird-cage from one of his parishioners. There was no doubt that the old man was delighted with his new pet, and as she left the cottage, Sarah felt that Christmas had really begun.

Sarah spent the rest of the morning with Peter, Benny and Dad, decorating the cottage with holly and paper chains. Mum was working all day at the fruit shop.

At lunchtime, Mum arrived home. "I can't stay long," she said, breathlessly. "We're so busy! You'd think that Christmas was going to last for a month, the way everyone's buying!" She hesitated in the doorway, one hand behind her back. "Now, you're not to laugh," she said, defensively.

Slowly, Mum produced her surprise. "I know it's not *quite* like the ones we've had before," she said, "but nobody wanted it, and Mary Crudge said I could have it for nothing."

"It *is* a bit small," Peter said doubtfully.

Benny just stared, and Dad chuckled. "The runt of the litter!" he laughed, putting an arm around his wife. "Well done, love. I'd decided that we couldn't afford one."

"Poor little thing," Sarah said, "it's a lovely little Christmas tree, Mum!" She examined the spindly branches, remembering the huge Christmas tree which, last year, had touched the ceiling in the lounge at Radford House.

"Oh look," she exclaimed, "it's much better than last year's – it's got roots. It might grow, if we plant it in the garden after Christmas."

Mother and daughter smiled understandingly at each other.

In the evening, after tea by the living room fire, the family turned out into the snowy night to go to the carol service at Wallington Church, and then they all walked round to Danny's field to give him his feed. The pony's dark shape showed up clearly against the snow, and he whinnied as they all walked away down the path.

Christmas day was all that it should have been, with presents, Christmas dinner and a snowy walk in the afternoon to feed Danny and to visit old Bill Codgers.

"It all goes to show," Sarah said, wryly, to her friend Min after Christmas, "That every silver lining has a cloud!"

Everything had seemed so perfect and happy at Christmas, that Sarah was totally unprepared for the shock of Min's news.

Min arrived on the 11 o'clock bus on the Saturday after Christmas.

As the bus came into sight, Sarah jumped down from the stile where she had been waiting, and there was Min, waving from inside.

"Hi!" said Min, jumping down from the bus, her haversack bouncing on her shoulder. "I'm on time for once!"

They chatted as they walked up the lane to Dogrose Cottage. Then, suddenly, Min stopped.

"I've got something awful to tell you," she said, slowly, "and I might as well get it over with."

"Oh Min," Sarah laughed, "don't be so dramatic!"

"I'm not," Min said, miserably, "I just don't want to tell you."

"Come on – what is it?"

Min hesitated. "It . . . it's Franny. She's had an accident."

Sarah's heart lurched.

"You know I said that Debbie had been hunting?"

Min said. Sarah nodded. Slowly, as they continued to walk up the lane, Min told her how Debbie and Franny had gone to the Boxing Day meet. "It wasn't Debbie's fault," Min said, "or Franny's, either. Neither of them could have seen the barbed wire. It was bundled up, just where Franny landed. Nobody knows how it got there – they think someone had been making an illegal snare. Anyway, Franny got caught up in it and then she fell against a barbed wire fence." Min stopped, looking at Sarah's white face.

"I think I've told you enough," she said, miserably. She stopped again, and turned towards Sarah. "I'm *terribly* sorry to have to tell you, but I *had* to. It's in the local paper today."

"Of course you had to," Sarah said, bleakly, looking straight ahead. "What – what happened?"

"Well, Debbie just fell off – she was all right. Some people stopped to help and one of them galloped off to fetch the vet who lived quite close. He came and worked on Franny's cuts right there in the field. Debbie thinks that he saved Franny's life – she was bleeding so much and he stitched her up as quickly as he could."

"It must have been bad, then."

"It was awful. I haven't seen her, though – she's at Langton Veterinary Hospital."

Sarah unclenched her hands and her stomach stopped churning over. "So – she *is* getting better," she asked Min, cautiously.

Min bit her lip, avoiding Sarah's eyes. "Ye–es. She's being treated at Langton," she replied, flatly.

"So – she *will* be all right, eventually?"

"Well – not exactly."

They had reached the gate of Dogrose Cottage. Sarah turned towards her friend. "Min, *please* tell me," she begged.

Min turned her eyes miserably towards Sarah. "She's going to be put down," she said, quietly. "The vet doesn't think that she will be able to be ridden again. Mr Hughes had her well insured. The Insurance Company have agreed to pay the full amount, and the vet's fees, but they're not willing to go on paying for her to stay on at Langton. Debbie can have a new pony with the insurance money."

"But they *can't*," Sarah said, angrily. "Not Franny. Doesn't Debbie *care* about her?"

"Well, yes, she does care," Min said, "but she's keen to have another pony to ride. It's very difficult," she added, lamely.

"Well, *I* wouldn't find it difficult," Sarah commented, scornfully, "I'd keep Franny and look after her."

Sarah paused at the back door. She looked at Min's troubled face. "Gosh, Min, I'm sorry. I'm shouting at you as if it's all your fault."

"I just can't stop feeling that Franny still belongs to me," she admitted, as she opened the door. "Come on – I'll try and forget about it."

Sarah took Min down to see Danny after lunch, and they went for a ride across the moors. Sally was confined to her bed with a sharp attack of flu.

"I can't let you up to see her, Sarah," Mrs Green said, when Sarah and Min called at the house.

"She's got a really high temperature – I don't want you to catch the flu just when you're starting a new school."

As Min and Sarah rode back towards Danny's field, the rain began. Soon it was pouring down, quickly washing away the remains of the Chirstmas snow – rather like, Sarah thought, Min's news had washed away the Christmas happiness. Hastily putting Danny back into his field with a plentiful supply of hay, the two girls cycled home through the driving rain.

"You two look almost as wet as I was when I arrived home!" Mrs Hinton greeted them, as Sarah and Min stepped into the hall and stood, dripping onto the tiles.

"Ugh! I must take my jeans off," Min said, "They're sticking to my legs."

"Come on," said Sarah, leading the way upstairs, "let's get changed."

Most of the rest of Min's stay was spent playing Ludo and listening to records, since the heavy rain continued, relentlessly.

Min went home on Sunday afternoon, leaving Sarah to wander restlessly about the cottage, trying desperately not to think about Franny. Eventually, she took herself off to bed early, where she tossed and turned, unable to sleep. She fell into a fitful sleep at last, in the early hours of Monday morning, to the sound of steady rain drumming on her window.

9

The Rescue

When Sarah awoke later on that morning, she wondered what was wrong. Then she realised – it wasn't raining!

She sat up in bed, rubbing her eyes sleepily. Smokey, asleep on the end of her bed, lifted his head and blinked. He yawned, delicately, and then tucked his nose in again between his paws.

"*I'm* not going to laze away the last days of the holidays," Sarah told him, sternly, as she scrambled out of bed. "I'm going to see Danny."

Suddenly, with a sinking feeling in the pit of her stomach, Sarah remembered what Min had told her. She sat on the side of her bed in her pyjamas, gazing at the photograph of Franny. Surely it couldn't be true? But she knew that what Min had told her must be true. Turning her gaze away, she stood up.

"I must stop thinking about Franny," she told herself, resolutely. "She doesn't belong to me any more and what Mr Hughes decides to do is none of my business."

The pale winter sunshine helped to dispel any depressing thoughts, and Sarah sang as she cycled down the lane and turned off towards the moors. It felt strange without Sally, who was still confined to bed.

"You're all mine today, Danny," Sarah told the little brown pony, as she buckled the headcollar and tied Danny to the gate. She fetched the dandy brush from her saddle-bag and began to brush the mud from Danny's thick winter coat. She brushed out his long black tail and thick, wayward mane, humming softly to herself as she worked. "There, little pony, you look better now," she told him, standing back to view her work, critically.

Sarah noticed with pleasure that Danny was beginning to fill out, losing the thinness in his flanks. Picking up the bridle from the gatepost, where she had hung it, Sarah put the reins over Danny's head. Then, unbuckling the headcollar, she slipped it off, replacing it with the bridle. Danny chewed on the cold metal, as the bit slipped into his mouth. Easing the headpiece round the pony's ears, Sarah buckled the throat-lash and pulled Danny's long forelock from under the headband.

"Come on, little Danny," Sarah said, slipping one arm through the reins while she opened the gate. "Let's go for our first ride of the year."

Sarah closed the gate. Then, gathering up the reins in her left hand, and making Danny stand, she put her two hands on his back and leapt up onto his bare back. Danny moved off, eager to be away, as Sarah wriggled into position on his back. Eagerly, Danny turned towards Moor Lane.

On an impulse, Sarah checked the little pony.

"No, Danny," she said, easing him round. "Let's go down the track, just for a change."

The cinder path which led from Moor Lane past Danny's field, grew narrower as it continued past Bill Codgers' cottage, becoming a narrow track which ran straight across the moor. It was disused now, and had become overgrown in places. Deciding to explore, Sarah urged Danny on, trotting and cantering down the grassy path. Coming to a place where a bush had grown right across the path, Danny stopped, snorting excitedly.

Sarah patted his neck. "That was a lovely canter," she told him, and then she turned her head to listen.

She could hear a pony somewhere, she was sure. It seemed to be whinnying gently, and yet each whinny ended with a grunt. It was a strange noise, and sounded somehow wrong. Sarah slipped down from Danny's back. Holding the reins near his head, she led him forward, pushing past the edge of the bush.

At first, Sarah could not see a pony, and then the strange whinnying grunt came again. Following the direction of the sound, Sarah let out a gasp. There, on her right, half way down the bank of the ditch, was Cassim, his eyes dilated with fear. His hind legs were almost completely submerged in the water, and each time he struggled to scramble out and up the bank, he seemed to sink further into the mud.

Sarah looked on, helplessly. What on earth could she do? She thought quickly, looking at the steep bank of the ditch. She could not possibly hope to be of any help to Cassim on her own.

"Hang on, Cassim, I'll be back," she called. She hated to leave him there, terrified and alone, but she must get help. Turning back and again pushing past the bush, she flung herself onto Danny's back and urged him on. Danny seemed to sense the urgency, as he galloped back along the track, his small hooves seeming to fly over the ground. Past the two cottages, they galloped and past Danny's field. Steadying him to a trot at the junction with Moor Lane, Sarah again urged him into a fast canter along the grass verge beside the river.

"I must save him, I *must,*" was pounding through Sarah's mind, in time with the thudding of Danny's little hooves on the grass. Cassim's beautiful Arab head, with its terrified eyes, was imprinted on her mind.

At last, Sarah could see the entrance to Moor End Riding Stables. She turned Danny into the entrance and they cantered over the bridge and into the yard. Sarah threw herself from Danny's back and flung the reins over the gatepost. No time now to worry about Danny jerking his head and breaking the reins.

Sarah found that her legs were trembling as she ran across the yard towards the stables. Surely, Mandy or Rob must be there? But the stables were deserted, and Sarah remembered that it was a bank holiday, and that Mandy had decided to have a break from giving riding lessons.

Sarah banged on the front door of the cottage. No reply – surely they weren't out? Near to tears, she looked desperately about her. The path continued round the side of the little, white-washed cottage and there, at last, through the french doors which led from the garden into the lounge, Sarah could see Rob. He was leaning back in an arm-chair, blissfully listening to a record. Sarah banged her knuckles sharply against the glass, and Rob sat up quickly. For what seemed to Sarah like minutes, Rob stared at her in amazement. Then, he leapt to his feet and hurried over to unlock the door.

"Whatever's the matter?" he asked, as Sarah tumbled in, pouring her story out in an unintelligible string of words. "Hey, wait a minute," Rob said, turning to switch off the record player. "Slow down a bit – perhaps I'll be able to hear you now."

"Cassim," Sarah panted. "He's stuck in a ditch – one of those huge, deep ones. He's in quite far already – it looks really bad."

Now, at last, Rob began to react. "You know where the feed room is?" he asked. Sarah nodded. "Well, hanging up at the back are a whole lot of ropes. Can you put them in the land-rover for me, please, while I go and wake Mandy – she's having a lie-down – and I'll phone a friend of mine to help." He ran his fingers through his hair, while he thought. "Where exactly is the ditch?" Sarah explained, and Rob nodded. "Right. Let's get going, then!" he said.

The journey back to to Cassim in the land-rover was a hair-raising experience. Having left Danny in a stable at Moor End, Sarah clung to the sides of her seat, between Rob and Mandy, as Rob, grim-faced and determined, drove at breakneck speed down the deserted lane, skidding round the corner into the cinder path. Mandy looked pale and anxious as she tried to question Sarah above the noise of the engine.

They reached the bush on the path, and Rob leapt out and ran round to the back of the land-rover. Pulling out the ropes, he pushed his way past the bush. Cassim seemed to have sunk even further into the muddy water. His hind quarters were almost completely submerged and his front legs were now in the ditch as well.

Mandy climbed down the steep bank and tried to soothe Cassim by talking to him, while Rob waded into the water with the ropes.

"What shall I do?" Sarah called.

"Catch the ropes when I throw them," Rob ordered. "I'm going to get them round his quarters."

Sarah was amazed to see how deep the water was in the ditch, as Rob waded in up to his shoulders in its murky depths. She realised, then, how serious the situation was.

Mandy's mud-splattered face looked anxious as she called out. "He's weak, Rob. He's been struggling for so long, he's worn out."

Rob looked grim. He passed the ropes around Cassim's hind quarters and threw them to Sarah, who waited at the edge of the water.

"Now take the two rope ends up the bank, Sarah. Is there a tree anywhere that you can loop them round?"

Sarah looked, but there was not even a bush nearby. "I'm afraid not," she said.

"Damn it," Rob muttered, "where on earth's Sid – he said he'd come straight away."

As if in answer, a tractor appeared, trundling slowly across the field, and a man wearing working clothes and Wellington boots, jumped down. He immediately took in the situation and looked troubled. "You're not going to save him," he said, grimly, "I've seen animals drown in these ditches in weather conditions like this."

"Come on," said Rob, ignoring his pessimism, "grab those ropes and tie them to the tractor. Then we'll pull him out."

This done, Sid revved up the engine of the tractor and put it into gear. The tractor moved forward, taking the strain of the ropes. Rob pushed on Cassim's quarters while Mandy, her arms round his neck, talked soothingly to him. Cassim, his front legs free of the water, struggled, trying to get a foothold, but all to no avail.

"OK! Stop a minute," Rob panted. He climbed out of the water and part way up the steep bank.

"Cassim's all in, Rob," Mandy said, "I think we ought to call Mr Clayton, the vet."

"Yes, I think you're right," Rob agreed.

"Well, I think your only hope is the fire brigade," Sid put in.

"Yes," Rob mused, "Perhaps *you're* right, too . . . Now, which of us can go?

Sarah looked at them; Mandy with her arms round Cassim's neck, doing her best to calm him; Rob, with his hands still on the all-important ropes; and Sid with the tractor holding the ropes taut.

67

"I'll go," Sarah said. "I can run back to that telephone box on the corner of Moor Lane."

Rob looked relieved. "Are you sure you can manage?" he said. Sarah nodded. "Well, Mr Clayton's number is 09384 – reverse the charges and explain to him what has happened. Can you manage the 999 call?

When Sarah thought about it afterwards, it seemed exciting, but at the time all she could think of was getting more help to Cassim as soon as possible. She delivered her messages in a shaky voice, first to Mr Clayton, the vet, who said that he would be over straight away, and then to the fire brigade. This second call took a little longer, since she also had to explain the situation to the police who said that they, too, would come. Sarah waited outside the telephone box and, within minutes, a police car arrived, followed shortly by the fire engine.

"Jump in, Miss," called a policeman, opening the back door of the car. "You're going to show us the way, aren't you?"

They sped down Moor Lane and turned down the cinder path, with the fire engine in hot pursuit.

"You couldn't have chosen a worse place," commented the police driver, as the car lurched down the track. The other policeman looked at Sarah, kindly. "Is it *your* pony that's stuck?" he asked.

"Oh, no," Sarah assured him, "but it's a valuable horse – an Arab stallion!"

"They're all the same to me, I'm afraid," the policeman chuckled, "just four legs, a head and a tail! Still," he added, nodding his head in the direction of the fire engine, "if anyone can get it out, those chaps will."

They stopped behind the land-rover and immediately the whole track seemed to be swarming with men. By the time Sarah reached the top of the bank, two of the firemen were already deep in conversation with Rob, while two others were running from the fire engine, carrying hosepipes. Sarah wondered how hosepipes could help, since there was no fire, but she was soon to learn.

Mr Clayton arrived on the scene. "Is he very exhausted?" he called to Mandy.

"*Very,*" Mandy replied. "I'm having to hold his head out of the water."

"Right. I'll be with you in a jiffy." Mr Clayton took a syringe from his bag. Turning to Sarah, he said "Can you bring my bag for me, please?" and then he began to climb down the bank.

"Now, hold him steady," he said quietly to Mandy. "Steady, boy," he added to Cassim, as he injected him in the neck. "That's an anti-shock injection," he explained, as he turned to reach into his bag, which Sarah held out for him. "Now we'll give him a stimulant." He injected Cassim again. "There," he said, "that ought to calm him down and give him some strength."

Meanwhile, several firemen were in the ditch. Now, Sarah could see that the hosepipes were to put round Cassim's quarters in place of the ropes, and also round his neck. The firemen tied the other ends to the tractor, and Sid again started the engine.

Cassim struggled and scrambled more strongly this time, but still they could not pull him free. He fell back, exhausted.

The team of rescuers gathered together, whilst Mandy and Rob remained with Cassim.

"It's that bank," said one of the men, "it's too steep. We've got to make a gentler slope of it – we'll use the axes."

They set to work with the axes, hacking at the steep bank. When they had hacked away a section of the bank, they fixed more hosepipes around Cassim's fetlocks.

"Now then, we're going to try again," called the chief fireman. "Take it steady with the tractor!"

"Please be careful," Mandy called. Sarah held her breath.

Slowly, the tractor moved forward, taking up the strain of the hosepipes. Rob, still shoulder high in the muddy water of the ditch, pushed on Cassim's hind quarters. The firemen and policemen added their strength, pulling on the hosepipes, looking, Sarah thought, like a one-sided tug o' war team. This time, slowly but surely, Cassim was hauled up the slope and at last, with a grunt, he struggled to his feet on dry land, as a small cheer rose from the rescuers.

10

A New Home

Cassim was a bedraggled sight as he stood with muddy water dripping from his coat. Mandy flung her arms around his neck, tears of relief running down her cheeks. The policeman and firemen gathered round.

"You can't imagine how grateful we are," Rob said, having scrambled up the bank after Cassim. He, too, was covered in mud.

"Yes, thank you all so much," Mandy added.

"We're only too glad to have been of assistance," the chief fireman said.

"Glad it was all successful," a policeman added.

Now that all the excitement was over, the rescuers began to disperse, gathering up the hosepipes and axes. Sarah suddenly realised how cold it was. Mandy, too, shivered. "I must get Cassim back to the stables," she said, looking towards the vet. "Is he all right, do you think?"

Mr Clayton felt Cassim carefully all over. Straightening up, he said, "Just a slight strain in that off hind leg, but otherwise he seems quite sound."

"Thank goodness," Rob murmured.

"I should get him back as soon as you can," Mr Clayton advised. "Get him rubbed down and in the warm."

"Come on then, old boy," Mandy coaxed, "back to your stable."

"I'll come with you," Sarah said.

Gently, Mandy led Cassim across the field. He was limping slightly. They walked in silence for a few moments; then Mandy spoke. "I'll never forgive myself for be so careless," she said.

"Why careless?" Sarah asked.

"I should have checked the fencing after that snow," Mandy explained, "and I should have realised, too, with all the rain we've had, that the ditches would be flooded and the banks slippery."

They walked through the gateway of the field. "And, you know, Sarah, I don't know how I shall ever be able to thank you," Mandy said, quietly.

"Why me?" Sarah replied, "I hardly did anything. We'd never have got him out without the firemen."

Mandy looked across at her. "I know," she said, "but just imagine what might have happened if you hadn't seem him and rushed to tell us."

Sarah shuddered. "I'd rather not think about it," she admitted, remembering Cassim's terrified eyes and how much further he had sunk into the water when she had seen him for the second time. She patted Cassim's mud-caked neck. "Thank goodness he's all right now," she added, fervently.

"Yes," Mandy agreed, "And it's all thanks to you, Sarah."

As she climbed thankfully into bed that night, Sarah turned over the events of the day in her mind. Thank goodness that Cassim was safe, she thought, sleepily, and then, with an ache in her heart, she remembered Franny. Too tired to think any more, she drifted off to sleep, with Franny and Cassim cantering through her dreams.

It was still dark, and Sarah's clock told her that it was only half past six when she woke up the next morning. She sat up in bed, suddenly wide awake, and not knowing why. She frowned, and tried to remember . . .

Then, at last, she *did* remember, and her heart quickened. Had it been a dream, or just the idea that had woken her? She didn't know and she didn't care. Hugging her thoughts to herself for a few minutes more, she sat in bed, gazing at the sky getting lighter and hoping, hoping . . .

Sarah switched on her bedside light and climbed out of bed. She must get dressed quickly and get on with it. Every minute was important. Shivering with excitement, and because of the cold morning, she opened her bedroom door quietly and padded along to the bathroom to wash and dress in her school clothes. The cottage was still asleep as Sarah crept down the stairs to the kitchen. Podge looked surprised to see her and gave her a sleepy welcome. "Walkies soon, Podge," she told him. She looked up at the clock. Perhaps she shouldn't telephone quite this early.

Sarah filled the kettle and put it on the Aga; then she set a tray for tea. By the time she had laid the

73

table for breakfast, the kettle was singing merrily, so she made the tea and carried the tray upstairs.

"You're up and about early," Mrs Hinton commented, sitting up in bed and looking sleepily at her daughter. "Is this a New Year's resolution? What a lovely surprise."

Sarah smiled. "No, I'm afraid not," she admitted, "I've just got . . . something to do."

Mum looked at her quizzically. "You must be looking forward to your new school," she said.

In the kitchen, the clock showed ten past seven. Sarah put on her coat, took 10p from the purse in her satchel, and clipped on Podge's lead.

A grey morning greeted them as Sarah and Podge stepped out of the back door and made their way down the path and then down the lane towards the telephone box.

Sarah felt a twinge of guilt as she heard the ringing tone continuing on and on. At last, a sleepy voice said "Hello," followed by the pips. Sarah pushed in her 10p and the pips stopped.

"Hello," she said, breathlessly, "I'm terribly sorry to telephone so early, but please can I speak to Min – it's Sarah."

"Well, yes, of course, Sarah." Mrs Cutler's voice sounded surprised. "Is anything wrong?"

"No," Sarah replied, "I just *must* speak to Min. It – it's rather important."

"Just a minute, then."

Sarah could hear Mrs Cutler calling Min. There was a long pause, and then Min's mother called again. Sarah chewed her lip, wishing that she had

had the sense to bring another 10p with her, just in case.

At last she heard Min's voice, heavy with sleep. "Hello, Sarah, is that *you?*"

"Yes. Min – are you awake yet? It's important."

"I think so," Min yawned.

"Min, listen," Sarah said, "I haven't much time before the pips and I haven't got another 10p. Can you *please* go and see Debbie on your way to school and ask her father not to do anything about Franny this morning – you said he would be deciding by the new year."

"Ye–es," Min still sounded sleeply. "But, I don't understand. Why are you –"

"Min, *please*," Sarah said, urgently, as the pips began, "I can't explain now, but please go and see Debbie's father – it's *very* important and –" Sarah stopped as the pips ended and the line went dead.

She looked down at Podge. "That's the first part done," she told him, and he wagged his tail encouragingly.

Mum was up when Sarah and Podge arrived back at the cottage, and an inviting smell of bacon and eggs filled the kitchen.

"I'm starving," Sarah announced, warming her hands against the Aga.

"I should think so," said Mum, "after early morning walks before breakfast."

Benny was running a plastic car up and down the backs of the kitchen chairs. He stopped and fixed his blue eyes on Sarah.

"Where have you been?" he demanded.

75

"Oh – just out," Sarah replied, vaguely.

"Why?" Benny persisted.

Mrs Hinton came to Sarah's rescue. "Now, Benny, stop pestering and come and have your breakfast," she said. She looked across the table with understanding in her grey eyes. Sarah returned the look gratefully.

"I'll tell you later, Benny," Sarah promised, "but just now I don't want to talk about it, in case it all goes wrong."

Eyeing the clock, Sarah said, "Can I have my breakfast, too, Mum. I've got to hurry."

Mrs Hinton looked puzzled, as she handed over a plate of eggs and bacon. "But school isn't until a quarter to nine – you've got an hour to spare," she said.

"Mm, I know," Sarah mumbled between mouthfuls, "but I've got to go down to the village first."

Mrs Hinton left her questioning there, understanding her daughter's need for privacy. "Well, don't be late on your first day, will you?" was all she said.

The milkman was whistling his way down the path with the empty bottles when Sarah left the cottage, five minutes later. She passed the milk float a few minutes later, as it clanked its way slowly down the lane. Sarah sped down towards the village and turned her bicycle into Moor Lane.

"He doesn't look as if anything had happened to him, does he?" said Sally, reaching up to stroke Cassim's shining chestnut neck. Cassim snorted

76

noisily and stretched his neck further out of the opening of his loose box door, to push his nose into Sally's pocket.

"He's so gentle," Sarah remarked, watching Cassim delicately accepting the piece of carrot that Sally had found for him. "I always thought that stallions were – well, wild and uncontrollable."

Sally laughed. "Not Cassim," she said. "He's just a great big softie!"

Just then, Mandy's voice called, "He's here!"

Sarah's heart beat faster as she turned away from Cassim's stable. Her eyes searched the lane and there, sure enough, was Rob, manouevring the horse box carefully over the little bridge which led into the stable yard. Sitting up beside Rob in the front was Min, grinning from ear to ear. Rob drove the horse box across the yard and brought it to a standstill in a quiet corner.

Sarah felt suddenly uncertain and she hung back as Sally hurried forward and Rob and Min jumped down from the cab. Mandy joined them, together with a little girl who had been brought early for her 11 o'clock Saturday morning ride.

"Here we go, then," said Rob, pulling back the bolts and letting down the ramp. He walked up the ramp and half a minute later appeared again, leading a beautiful strawberry roan. The pony walked carefully and stiffly down the ramp, her long mane lifting slightly in the breeze.

Now, Sarah wanted to be with the others, to help Franny down the ramp and to pat her and welcome her to her new home. She hurried forward.

Mandy smiled at her, understanding how Sarah felt, for it was the same feeling that she had for Cassim.

"Come on, Sarah," she said, "you take her into the loose box and make her feel at home." She saw Sarah's eyes fill with pain when she looked at Franny's scarred legs and neck, where the stitches had not yet been removed. "We'll get to work on those cuts with salt and water," she said. "If we bathe them every day, they'll soon heal."

Sarah found her hands trembling as she reached out to hold the headcollar and to rub Franny behind the ears. Franny looked at her with her lovely, liquid brown eyes, and she nudged Sarah gently, just as she always used to.

"She remembers you!" said Min. Sarah felt tears of happiness stinging her eyes as she led the pony carefully across the yard and into the loose-box.

When she had settled Franny and watched her for a while as she pulled at the hay from her hay net, Sarah let herself quietly out of the stable. Sally and Min were over by the gate, where Danny waited, patiently.

"She *is* lovely, isn't she," said Sally.

"Thank goodness you managed to persuade Mandy to have her here," Min added.

"I didn't need to persuade her," Sarah explained. "As soon as I told her about my idea of keeping Franny here for breeding, she got *really* excited and went off to telephone Mr Hughes straight away."

"She's here on permanent loan, isn't she?" Min asked.

Sarah nodded. "Mr Hughes said that he couldn't sell her because he has had the insurance money, so Mandy pays for all her keep on the understanding that she will own any foals that Franny has. With Cassim being Arab and Franny half-Arab, they should have some lovely foals."

"Don't you wish she belonged to you again?" Sally queried.

"Of course I do, but we can't possibly afford to keep her," Sarah replied, "and this is the next best thing. Anyway, the important thing is that she won't be put down."

Sally laughed. "Look at us," she said, "you with Franny to love and look after, and me with Cassim, but neither of us with a pony of our own to ride."

"But you're both lucky," Min broke in, "you've got Danny."

Danny obviously agreed, for he shook his thick brown mane and snorted, impatiently.